HAPPY BROOMSTICK DAY

written by Pauline Mackay

illustrated by Marjory Tait

Ablekids Press

For *The Boglashin Boys,* Christopher, Craig and Jamie. In memory of *Witchy Pooh!* P.M.
To Erik, Floki and Ivar. Thank you for being my inspiration. M.T.

Published by Ablekids Press Ltd
46 Ballifeary Road
Inverness
IV3 5PF
Scotland

www.ablekidspress.com

Text © 2019 Pauline Mackay
Illustration © 2019 Marjory Tait

ISBN 978-1-910280-36-2

Typeset by Bassman Books

Printed in Scotland by Bell & Bain Ltd

British Library Cataloguing-in-Publication Data
A catalogue record for this book is available from the British Library

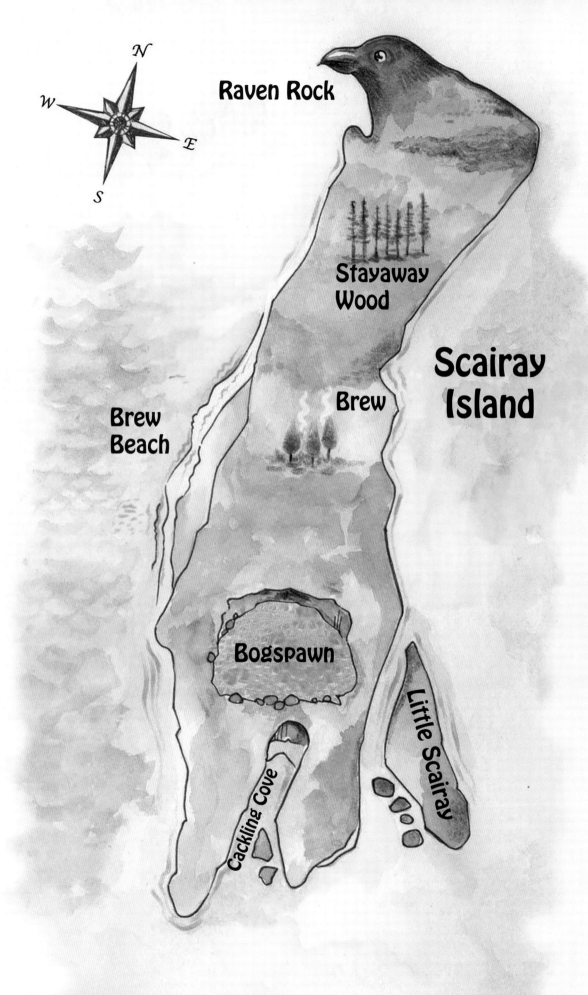

Raven Rock

Scairay Island

Stayaway Wood

Brew

Brew Beach

Bogspawn

Cackling Cove

Little Scairay

N
W
E
S

The village of Brew, on the island of Scairay, was celebrating its 500th annual Broomstick Day. Black bunting fluttered merrily in the breeze and hearty cackles rose from market stalls where witches were selling hats, jewellery, potion bottles and wands.

Spellbound, the bookshop, was packed with fans of Verilee Warty who was reading from her bestseller, *Broomsticks Have Feelings Too!* Other popular titles such as *Celebration Spells* and *The Meaning of Miaow* were flying out the door.

In The Sticky End, Guzzle the Baker was trying to keep up with demand for her festive cauldron cakes, wormiferous webs and bug-free biscuits.

Later in the day, there was going to be a parade of vintage broomsticks. Then, the fiercely contested cat 'n' wand race and three-handled race. Finally, the winner of the *Hag Stick*, for the most original broomstick, would be announced.

Everyone was buzzing with excitement. Well, almost everyone. Greta didn't receive *Happy Broomstick Day* greetings. Nor did she ever take part in the yearly celebration. Why not? It was very simple.

Greta was allergic to broomsticks.

This was definitely NOT GOOD for a witch. Regardless of drinking the foulest concoctions and covering herself in stinking creams, no potion or lotion made one bit of difference.

A broomstick of Ash brought her out in a rash
And patches of bubbling blue spots;
A broomstick of Oak turned her voice to a croak
And tied her tongue tightly in knots.
A broomstick of Lime changed her skin into slime,
All squidgy and sticky and green.
A broomstick of Alder? That left her balder
Than any witch she'd ever seen!
A broomstick of Beech made her swell like a peach,
Until she was dark red and round;
A broomstick of Larch bent her into an arch
And rooted her hands to the ground.
A broomstick of Pine drew out spikes from her spine
That curled to the tip of her nose;
A broomstick of Fir meant she started to purr
And sharpen the claws on her toes.

In desperation, Greta had tried other ways of flying around – all ending rather disastrously.

A sympathetic Scairay witch, living in a far-off land, sent her a dragon. At first, Greta was grateful but it kept setting her on fire.

Also, there was the small matter of having to save her cat from being eaten. Greta would never believe the dragon was just playing! It really had to go back.

But worse was to come!

Flying spells from *The Book of Crones* were only supposed to be used on broomsticks, but the discovery of an abandoned cauldron on Brew Beach had given the young witch an idea. Greta squeezed into the frogsmelly pot and cast an ancient spell. The rusty vessel rocked violently, then carried off its helpless cargo, bouncing mercilessly across the rolling waves.

A neighbour, who was gathering driftwood, heard her screeches and raised the alarm. Rescuing her from the mutinous cauldron had not been easy.

But worse was to come!

One day, on her way home from Raven Rock, Greta unwisely took a shortcut through Stayaway Wood. A hunched-up little goblin was sitting on a log by the path. Goblins always brought trouble so Greta pretended she hadn't seen him.

"And that's why I'm so sad!" wailed the goblin. "Nobody stops to talk. Lonely me."

"What about your friends? Where are they?" The words slipped out of Greta's mouth without thinking.
"No friends," he replied.

Tears welled up in Greta's eyes.

"Where are your friends?" asked the wily goblin.
"No friends," sobbed Greta.
"No friends!" repeated the goblin with a sly smile.

Greta explained why she couldn't join in with the other witches.
"But they laugh at me and call me *The Walking Witch*."
"Well, I might be able to help," said the goblin with a glint in his eye. "Meet me here at the same time tomorrow."

And even though Greta should have known better, that is exactly what she did.

The goblin was waiting impatiently. He pulled a white, feathery bundle from his sack and smiled from ear to ear.
"These are for you. Pegasus wings. Let me help you with them. Now turn around three times to make the magic work. Believe me, nobody will call you *The Walking Witch* again!"

Oh dear! If only Greta had stopped to think! If only she had heeded the warning:

> Goblin tricks are never fun.
> Goblin smiles should make you run.
> Stayaway's a goblin wood
> And goblins don't do any good!

Greta squealed with delight as the Pegasus wings stretched open and started to flap.

Soon she was whizzing over Brew Beach with a crowd of astonished witches following her. What a sight!

But Greta's joy didn't last long.

By the time she reached Bogspawn, the wings felt strange and uncomfortable.
It was only when she tried to land that Greta remembered the goblin's final words:

Nobody will call you *The Walking Witch* again!

The Pegasus wings, now as black as the darkest night, would not allow Greta's feet
to touch the ground. At first, the other witches laughed and teased her. Then they
discovered the awful truth. The wings were a goblin gift.

Poor Greta spent months perched in trees until the oldest witch on Scairay cooked up a spell powerful enough to dissolve the wicked goblin's magic and remove the enchanted wings.

So, on the 500th anniversary of Broomstick Day, when all the island witches were out celebrating, Greta remained at home, alone with her cat.

A knock at the door made her jump. No-one was there. Instead, she found a long parcel with a label saying:

Special Present from Somewhere Hot

Love Aunt Flora xxx

Greta smiled for the first time that day.
Her aunt often sent unusual presents
from her travels around the world. Some
were a little dangerous, so she was glad
the parcel began to unwrap itself.

There was also a letter.

Darling Gretchy,

I think I have solved your problem
and the answer is ... BANANAS!

I discovered this
wonderful plant
growing on a
tropical island.
It looks like a
tree – but isn't one!

I have made you a new
broomstick, which whistles
sweetly in the wind.
Don't be afraid!
Try it out.

Lots of love,
Aunt Flora

Greta gulped. There was no telling what effect this exotic present could have on her and she wasn't feeling lucky.
"One last experiment," she said to her cat. "If anything goes wrong, I'll never touch another broomstick!"

The Scairay witches couldn't believe their eyes when Greta swooshed into the tent where the Hag Stick competition was being judged. A great cheer went up when ...

NOTHING HAPPENED!

A second cheer greeted the surprise winner of the Hag Stick –
for her groundbreaking banana broomstick.

Happy Broomstick Day, Greta!
Happy Broomstick Day, indeed!

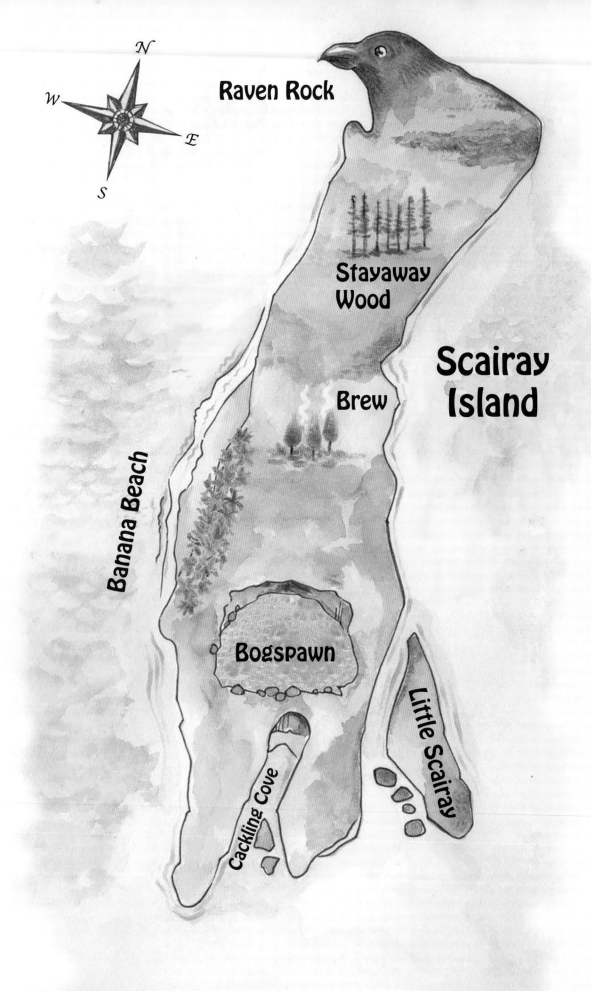